CREEPERS

To: Abigail

By Michael Finklea
Cover illustration by Vickie Sissel

Ozark Publishing
3020 N.E. 32nd. Avenue, Suite 1116
Fort Lauderdale, FL 33308

Contents

Don't You Want to Play?

Wolves were howling on the radio when my dad turned it on. A lady with a soft voice spoke. *"You've tuned into KWOLF. Your Timberwolf forecast starts with a twenty percent chance of rain."*

"Carol, it's not going to rain." I heard Dad correcting Mom. "What time did you tell her we would be there?"

"Now for the news. It's been a quiet day across the county . . ."

"Nobody talk to Luke," Laura jabbered. "He's finally about to fall asleep."

Tuning my sister out, I listened back to the lady on the radio. Her voice sounded a whole lot better than my sister's!

Suddenly the van jolted.

A huge *THUMP* under the right wheels caused our van to rock to its side.

Mom screamed, "Mike! Watch out!"

"Hold on!" Dad yelled, slamming on the brakes and spinning our van to the left.

Skidding across the gravel, we stopped just as the front wheels slid to the edge of a trench.

"Dad, what did you hit?" I asked, searching out the back window.

"You should have seen it, Luke," Laura said as she crumbled down into the seat. "It looked like some kind of gigantic flying bug!"

SPLAT!

All of a sudden, a huge black insect flew right into the front windshield. Bright green gunk burst out of its crushed shell, gushing across the window into thick streaming lines.

"Look at them." Mom's voice quivered.

I stared out the window in shock!

Huge scorpion like beetles with pinchers and long stingers were swarming right outside our van!

Dad yanked the gearshift in reverse and floored it as rocks shot forward into the darkness.

Throwing the van back in drive, Dad punched the accelerator, and we peeled out.

Big green splotches spattered across the front window as we plowed ahead scattering the huge bugs in our path.

"**MOM!**" Laura suddenly called out.

My head spun around to see that Laura's window was still down!

"Roll your window up!" I demanded.

Dad quickly released the front window locks and ordered Laura to get her window up.

"It won't go up!" She cried out, stabbing at the button. "It's stuck!"

Mom's face twisted in fear.

Tears were running down Laura's face as she screamed, "**Help me, Luke! Get it off me! It's got ahold of my leg!**"

My whole body froze! I just sat staring at one of the long-legged insects that was prying its way into Laura's window!

Then, without thinking, I took my hand and with one hard swat, I slapped it off her.

Its spindly legs broke off as it tore from her jeans. Its longest front leg dropped onto the floorboard below my sister's feet!

"**Stomp it!**" I ordered her.

Laura's foot cracked down on its crusty leg. It sent out green goop spraying into the air!

Suddenly we both let out a piercing scream!

"It's off you!" I yelled at her.

"Look!" she cried out, pointing down.

My eyes skipped off her and down to the floorboard.

An army of little green spiders began springing out of the bug's broken-off leg!

Little green spiders that were unrolling long stingers! Little green spiders that started marching in rows up Laura's legs!

Laura let out a blood-curdling scream as she began flicking the spiders off of her as fast as she could.

My stomach was churning with panic!

"Something's got ahold of my heel!" Mom yelled, grabbing at Dad's arm for help.

I saw the bristled legs of another one of the hideous black bugs that somehow got inside.

I looked back at Laura in terror!

She had gone from flicking off the spiders to pounding them into her jeans with the palms of her hands!

Doomed! I turned to my window.

Thousands of insects were diving at the van trying to sink their razor-sharp stingers into us!

Suddenly, the van began vibrating.

Then it began jerking harder and harder.

Our van was being forced to a crawl.

Mom and Dad stared at each other.

"It's going to be okay," Dad whispered.

But I could tell by the look in their eyes, things were not going to be okay.

The spiders were now prying their way into Laura's ears and mouth, spinning their webs around her horrified, ghostly white face!

"Dad!" I cried out pushing myself as far away from Laura as possible.

I reached up and put my hand on my mom's shoulder.

Mom's hand reached up and covered mine.

Then she reached over and touched Dad's cheek.

Mom's hand tightened over mine, so tight it hurt. "Mom!" I cried out lowly.

Then she jerked my hand forward.

It felt like she was going to pull my arm right out of its socket!

"M-Mom," I stuttered. "You're hurting me!"

She was squeezing my hand way too hard.

Suddenly her head spun around.

But the face I looked into was not my mom's.

Mom had disappeared.

Instead of my mother, I sat staring into the hollowed eyes of a rotted skeleton!

The skeleton lurched forward, and through its blackened teeth, I could feel the stench of its bad breath on my face.

"Don't you want to play?" it rasped.

Then it threw its skull back in a cackle of laughter.

Stranded in the Van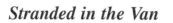

"Luke, wake up."

"I DON'T WANT TO PLAY!"

My eyes slammed open. Wide!

I saw that I was lying on the floorboard.

My whole family was staring at me.

Shaking, I pressed my hands against my chest. My heart was pounding so hard, I thought it was just going to bust right out.

"Luke, I'm not going to tell you again," Mom said, slapping her armrest. "Stop kicking the back of my seat. And get off the floorboard."

With her greasy finger, Laura reached over and poked me in the neck.

"Stop it! Why are you poking me?" I snapped back, wiping the chicken grease off the side of my neck.

"You're freaking out in your sleep, weirdo," Laura said, throwing her half-eaten chicken leg out the window. "What don't you want to play?"

Climbing back up into the seat, I tried to control my spastic breathing.

I saw that I had slid right out of my seat belt.

It took a couple of seconds before it hit me.

It had all been just a dream!

I looked back out the window. I didn't see any bugs. No giant black bugs.

That was a relief!

Then I checked the floorboard under Laura's feet.

There was nothing there, either.

"Instead of what you don't want to play, how about a game of Eye-Spy?" mom said, holding up a sticky note.

It had an address written on it.

"Yes." Dad agreed. His eyes darted from one side of the road to the other. "We can't find the house. Look for anything with *Scurlock Manor* written on it."

"Wanna play?" Laura asked, sucking in her greasy little cheeks, making a ridiculous fish face.

I studied her silly expression.

Then I studied her curly brown hair — fully expecting to see a spider stick his head out and wave.

Taking another deep breath, I answered, "No. I don't *wanna* play. There's nothing to spy out there anyway. It's just the same old dead trees that were there before I fell asleep."

"Just play the dumb game." Laura groaned and rolled her eyes at me.

"Okay, Eye Spy a giant beetle bug with red eyes munching on your head," I charged back.

"Dad . . . " Laura whined.

"Well. That's what my dream was about. Giant bugs attacking the van. Grabbing Laura! I even knocked one off of her."

I turned back to my annoying sister. "Better be nice to me, or next time I'll let them get you. That is, if you don't gross them out first."

Kicking my legs and stretching hard, I pushed deep into the back of my seat.

Mom's arm came sliding between the front seat and the passenger door.

Then came the pinch.

"*Ouch!*" I hollered out, rubbing my leg. "Why did you do that?"

"I said . . . quit kicking the back of my seat!"

I couldn't believe Mom got me that time.

I could usually spot her hand lurking in the shadows of the seat.

It was always like a snake ready to strike.

Looking up, I saw *another pair* of red eyes watching me.

It was Dad in the rearview mirror.

"Luke, I'm about to . . ." he started.

"Do it!" Laura cheered.

"Stop!" Mom yelled slapping the dashboard. "Well, I have an Eye Spy."

"Where?" Dad and Laura called out, looking in different directions.

"There," Mom said as she pointed to a thick patch of overgrown bushes and weeds at a small sign. You had to turn your head almost sideways to read it.

It was the sign for the house we had been looking for.

"How was anybody suppose to see that?" I asked as we all tilted our heads to the left.

Scurlock Manor was carved into the rotted wood. It looked like the old vines twisting around the little stick post were the only things holding it up.

Dad quickly jerked the wheel to the left.

The sun was going down as we drove up the long, bumpy driveway.

As the trees cleared I got my first look at the house that had taken us all day to drive to.

The house that kept me *stranded* in the van for all that time.

The house that my parents said we might buy.

And, an old, skinny woman who was waiting for us on the front steps.

"Who's that?" I asked, watching the woman tap her feet on the concrete steps.

Laura flicked the side of my ear. "She's the real estate lady, dummy."

"She's here. We're late," Mom said pulling the rearview mirror to her side then pinching her cheeks.

I always wondered why she did that. Pinch her cheeks, I mean. She always grabbed the mirror. Dad hated that.

Laura nudged me. "It makes them rosy."

"You would never see a soldier doing that," I informed her as I tied my official military bandanna above my ears.

I did not like a girl reading my mind, especially my sister.

Dad reached over and pulled the mirror away from Mom.

He positioned it so he could see both of us. "I want both of you to be on your very best behavior. This house is filled with very old antiques. The people who used to live here left everything when they moved out. Make sure you keep your hands where they belong. And take that thing off your head, Luke."

"Grandpa gave me this," I argued back.

Dad flashed me *the look.*

That meant — watch it!

Oh, and agree with anything he says.

Well, actually it meant a lot of different things.

Old Ms. Scurlock

It began thundering as I watched my parents cross the yard to meet the stranger.

Laura and I decided to hang out in the van for a little while longer. You know — waiting on the adults to finish their *how do you dos.*

I was waiting for Laura to finish putting on her jacket anyway. I was always waiting on her.

Laura's the kind of sister that most guys probably cringe about. You see, we're twins.

Mom says we're a lot alike.

We both have curly brown hair. That's my dad's fault, though. His hair is super curly, too.

In fact, we look exactly like our dad.

Mom's hair is long, straight, and bright red.

Dad thinks it's really funny — not Mom's hair, but how Laura and me look just like him.

Today I had another problem, though.

Even bigger than having a twin sister.

Even bigger than having a freaky nightmare about huge scorpion beetles!

Today, our dad was looking for another house for us to move to and fix up.

That was my dad's job, to move into old run-down houses and make them look good.

We've moved a lot over the years. But I hated moving, mostly because I end up having to work as hard as my dad.

He calls me his right-hand man.

I guess that's suppose to make me want to help out more. But it doesn't.

Still waiting on Laura to clean herself up, I stared over her head out the van.

I could hear the thunder, but I couldn't see a cloud in sight.

Turning back to my window, though, I saw them. Big black clouds that were rolling in fast.

Thunder rumbled again.

They were long rumbles that growled.

The black clouds were rolling around and smashing into each other. It was like they were assuming attack positions, growling like they were marking their territory.

Then a scream from Laura startled me.

I whirled around to see a big gust of wind rip the van door right out of her hands.

As the wind came lashing inside, it jerked the sticky note right off the dashboard.

It was the note Mom brought with the address of the house written on it.

It looked like a little magic carpet as it swooped up and down, zoomed around, and performed amazing loops and spirals.

Then with one clean jerk, it soared right out of the door.

"Hurry up, you guys! It's about to pour!" Mom called from the front porch.

"Move," I told Laura, pushing her out of my way. "What are you waiting on?"

"Look how big and old it is!" she said.
Her eyes were bulging more than usual.

I jumped out and stared up at the run-down place myself.

She was right. It *was* big. And old. *Really old.*
It looked like a giant brick skull.

Big columns, cracked and peeling, lined the front. Empty dark windows stared out from behind them. The windows reminded me of eyes. The columns reminded me of bones that were decaying and rotting.

Suddenly, a strong gust of wind stole my bandanna — ripping it right off my head — then sent it sailing through the air.

I watched as one of the upper-most branches of a dead tree snagged it — right before it cleared the tall brick chimney on the roof of the house.

As it hung there whipping in the wind, I noticed the black clouds were now above us.

They were quickly weaving a thick, dark blanket across the sky.

Then — like a dagger — the blackest cloud hurled a lightning bolt.

"I've never seen a storm come up so fast," Dad said as we came sliding across the porch.

Mom grabbed both of us by our shoulders and positioned us side by side.

We both held out our right hands and looked up and smiled.

"Who do we have here?" the stranger asked as she slowly turned to face us, her thin, gray lips curling into a smile.

"AH!" We both yelped.

Laura and I looked nervously at each other.

Thunder crackled, and rain began to pound the sidewalk like tiny little sledgehammers.

"These are our two darling children, Luke and Laura," mom said, clamping down on our shoulders and preventing us from making any sudden moves.

Mom motioned to her mouth for us to smile.

"Luke and Laura are twins. They just turned ten years old."

I couldn't say a word. I just stood staring up at the old woman and the deep, chiseled lines in her puckered-up face.

Wobbling on warped pencil legs, the old woman slowly removed her black gloves.

Then she held out her bony hand, her frizzy hair whipping around like hundreds of spindly snakes.

"Ms. Scurlock will be showing us the house," Dad said, smiling.

It took another minute for either of us to say anything.

Finally, Laura stuttered a hello and her name and quickly shook the woman's hand.

As fast as she shook it, she jerked it back and wiped her hand on her jeans.

Even though the old woman reminded me of human bat, I stood up straight and saluted her military style.

I informed her my name was Luke Conners.

I didn't like agreeing with my sister, but this time, I had to.

The woman's hand was ice cold and wet.

I wiped my hand off, too.

"Aren't you the charming little soldier?" she said, studying me with black beady eyes.

"One day I will be. A soldier, I mean."

As I lowered my salute, she lurched forward and muttered something into my ear.

I jumped back.

It was raining so hard, I couldn't understand what she said, though.

I looked at Laura and shrugged.

Laura yelled into my ear, "she said she's been expecting you."

Expecting me?

"We've been waiting for this day for a long time," she said as her shaky fingers battled with the key to get it inside the lock.

Without moving her body, she slowly turned only her head back to face me. "I was speaking of the rain, of course."

Her head almost seemed to be turned too far around to still be attached to her body.

Scurlock Manor

A thick bolt of lightning shot sideways across the sky — perfectly horizontal — as old Ms. Scurlock turned the key in the lock.

As the bolt slid back, it made a horrible moaning screech.

It sounded like she had wounded it.

As many times as I had looked at houses with my dad, I had never heard that before.

With the same strange smile, she threw her arms wide in the air. "Just look!" she called out, shoving both heavy doors open.

As the old, creaking doors swung back, only darkness greeted us.

That was okay by me. I wasn't sure what I was going to see.

By the looks of the house, I expected bats to come spilling out — or even worse, some of those swarming bugs in my dream!

But it was only darkness.

"This house is over a hundred years old. It was built in 1865," The scarecrow woman explained as we all stepped in.

"*Scurlock Manor.* Must be difficult letting go of a house that's been in your family for so long," Dad said, tapping his fingers together.

"Did you help build this house?" I asked.

"Heavens no." She laughed, tossing her large head back, her hair still whipping around. "My goodness, Luke. Honey, that would make me over one hundred and thirty years old."

I bobbed my head back and forth. I was still waiting, not sure of her answer.

"I apologize for my son," Mom declared as she threw her hand over my mouth.

I didn't appreciate that.

I didn't see a problem with my question.

"No, little soldier." She kept laughing. "We just happened to have the same last name."

"Spooky!" Laura said, tugging my coat.

"Totally," I agreed. "With that big head and skinny body, she looks kind of like a bug."

"Yeah," Laura whispered back. "She looks like some kind of giant stick bug."

She was right, I thought.

She did look like a giant stick bug.

The woman looked at me. I tried to smile.

"I understand this is a hobby of yours?" she asked Dad as she led him back out to the porch.

Yep, she was one creepy woman.

She stopped talking to Dad and turned around and looked right at me.

I wasn't sure, but it looked like she snarled.

"What's that back there hanging?" Laura asked Mom in a low voice.

Hanging?

I quickly ran back to Mom and squinted to see for myself.

Mom whispered to Laura, "I think it's a chandelier, honey."

"Yes, Mrs. Conners. It is a priceless old chandelier — a crystal one," Ms. Scurlock interrupted.

The old stick bug had heard Mom's whisper.

She had heard it from outside on the porch!

"Please, everyone," she said as she walked back in, "wait for me here. I must go down in the basement. I'll have the lights on in a jiffy."

"Why don't you let me go or at least go with you," Dad offered.

"Wait here." She repeated herself as her bony hand tweaked my nose.

I quickly jerked away from her clutch.

"Be a good little soldier and pick that up for me, please." She smiled the same frozen smile.

Trying not to take my eyes off her for too long, I quickly glanced down. There was a tall, thin candlestick in the corner where I was standing. I reached down and grabbed it.

Pulling a box of matches from her pocket, she said, "Please, hold it still for me to light."

"Oh my!" She let out a hideous laugh. *"Luke be nimble. Luke be quick. Luke is going to help me light my candlestick."*

I stared up into her beady eyes, confused.

Dad even looked a little creeped out.

"I'll be back before you can say BOO!" she said, snapping her bony fingers together.

Huddled together, we all watched her scurry away holding the candlestick with both shaky hands.

Scurrying along on pencil-thin legs.

Scurrying along into the darkness.

"Do you think she'll be okay?" Mom asked as she disappeared into the blackness.

"Oh. I have a feeling she will be," Dad answered, squinting and looking around the room. "She may look frail, but I have a feeling she knows how to take care of herself."

I thought that was kind of funny, but something told me he was probably right.

"Remember what Dad said. Keep your hands where they belong," Laura said, poking me in the neck again.

I didn't bother responding.

"Is something wrong?" Mom asked me.

She must have been *really* surprised when I didn't give my sister what she deserved!

Instead, I just stared around the dark room.

"It's like a standoff, you know."

"Oh brother. Here he goes again." Laura laughed.

I threw her a sneer and continued. "It's like a standoff between the fresh air outside and the musty forces inside this old abandoned crypt. Even the air that pushed past us when she opened the doors has now stopped dead in its tracks."

Laura dropped to the ground laughing.

About five minutes later, the old woman finally reappeared.

With another swing of her skinny arm, she flicked on a light switch. "Behold!"

"Yikes!" Laura jumped.

Thousands of spider-spun cobwebs were wrapped around everything in sight.

I saw a batch of large black ones scurry up the chain of the light and disappear into a crack in the ceiling.

I tried warning Laura again.

"I would be on guard if I were you. A siren has sounded in spider land. They're probably manning their battle stations. Hundreds of troops of deadly spiders awakened from a deep sleep."

Laura whispered back. *"You're a freak!"*

As Ms. Scurlock walked away, she let out a gruesome laugh. Tossing her large head back again, she giggled. "Don't worry, little ones. They don't bite . . . *much.*"

After that, I made up my mind not to talk to Laura for the rest of the day.

Or to stand too close to anything where deadly spiders could lurk.

Besides, we were on their turf!

We'll Take It!

As we walked through the small entryway into the main room, everyone kept in single file. I knew it wasn't just me. No one wanted to get too close to anything.

I took an extra step to get a little closer to Dad as we all made our way to the middle of the huge and oversized room.

The ceiling of the room went all the way up to the second story.

A wide staircase started on the right side and swung left, winding its way all the way up.

"It's beautiful! Isn't it?" Ms. Scurlock's voice whispered through the room.

I turned back to the door where she had been standing. She wasn't there.

She suddenly reappeared walking slowly down the big white marble staircase.

"How did she get all the way up there?" Laura asked Mom.

Mom answered, "Yes. It is beautiful!"

Covering my nose, I thought, beautiful?

The whole place was a big junk pile. And it smelled like nasty gym socks that had been pulled off a two-hundred-year-old dead person!

How could she say beautiful?

"Go on. Have a look around." Ms. Scurlock motioned with her claw-like hands.

Mom and Laura took off running in different directions.

"Be careful," Dad warned after them.

Laura shot off up the staircase to the second floor and disappeared from sight.

Mom headed toward the back of the house.

Dad left the room down a dark hallway.

I realized it was just me and *her* left in the room *alone* — us and the eerie cloud of dust hovering.

Passing by me, she whispered, "Not another *living soul* has been in here in thirty years."

The way she said *"living soul"* sent waves of shivers up my spine!

"It's time to breathe new life into the old place," she said loudly — like she was trying to make sure everyone could hear her.

Then she smacked a wasp with the back side of her hand and waved the dust out of her face.

Letting out a huge sneeze, I blurted out, "What's that smell?"

Wiping her finger across the banister rail, she said, "Memories that have turned to dust, and probably many dead varmints, too."

Dad stepped back in and frowned at me. "Luke, no one has lived here for thirty years. It's been locked up for a long time."

He checked to make sure Ms. Scurlock was not listening. "If we buy this one, it's going to need a lot of work. That means lots of help from you, sport."

I now felt really sick to my stomach.

Had my family gone crazy?

I would be dead before it looked normal!

Then he left me alone again in the big room.

"It looks like it's just you and me, Luke. You should have a look around after you're moved in. Especially in the basement. I think there's an old trunk full of old army clothes, helmets, and such down there."

"Really?" I asked limp faced.

That *should* have sounded like good news.

Instead, I got a bad feeling in the pit of my stomach. It was the same feeling I got when I was doing something I wasn't suppose to be doing. Or, being someplace I wasn't suppose to be.

Didn't matter. I knew Dad was about to come to his senses.

Then we could finally get out of here.

To avoid hanging out with the human stick bug any longer, I decided to just wait for everyone outside on the front porch.

Two hours later, everyone finally came walking out!

I looked over my shoulder at Dad.

My biggest fear came true when he asked Mom the worst question I could think of.

"Carol, what do you think?"

Mom lowered her head and walked to the far side of the porch.

I knew my whole life was about to change when Mom swung around with a huge smile on her narrow face. She threw her arms up into the air and said, "We'll take it!"

Wolf Elementary

Two weeks passed. We were all moved in.

It was the fastest move we had ever made.

Mom and Dad had decided to keep all of the old furniture that was already in the house.

Dad sold all of our furniture to the people who bought our house.

I was finished fixing up my room. It was the only room I cared about, and I liked it.

After a lot of promising to help Dad, he let me paint it green. Army green!

Mom wasn't happy about it, but I liked it.

Laura painted her room putrid pink.

It looked like a big jar of Pepto Bismal.

I told her Pepto was suppose to make your stomach feel better. Walking into her room made me feel like puking!

We had also started our new school.

It's huge — one of the biggest elementary schools in the entire United States.

There's something like over 3,000 students!

They say the school has the most twins of any other school, too.

It's called Wolf Elementary.

Laura was busy making new friends.

I wasn't, though. At least not yet.

I'm still hoping Dad changes his mind and decides the house will take too much work.

I guess I really don't mind the school.

I like all the teachers, but there's something bugging me about living in that house.

"I've got a strange feeling about living here," I told Mom at dinner that night.

"It's called an intuition," she said, laughing. "Women get them, not ten-year-old boys."

"Well, whatever you call it, I'm getting one," I insisted.

Dad wasn't paying any attention to us.

He was busy spearing carrots and placing them on the edge of his plate. He hates carrots.

"Where's my napkin?" He suddenly broke out of his trance. His wrinkled forehead raised up from his plate.

I could see he was thinking hard about something. That usually meant more work.

Mom shook her head. "You know, Mike, if you would eat your carrots, you could see it."

"Don't be a smarty." He grunted. "Don't forget, I need everyone's help this weekend."

I knew it. I was right.

"Sorry, Dad." Laura smiled. "I told you already. Saturday's my track meet."

I could see Laura was up to her old tricks.

Then Mom said, "I won't be here, either."

She was up to her old tricks, too.

Dad turned to me.

"I can't, either." I began fidgeting around.

"Stop right there, sport," he said, pushing away from the table. "You definitely don't make any plans. I'm going to need your help."

Laura pushed her chair back and grinned. "Too bad. Here, wanna play my Game Boy?"

"Yeah. Give it to me," I grumbled.

"You didn't say the magic word."

"Toad!" I snorted. "That's the magic word. Then I'm going up to the attic to look around."

"No, you're not," dad said, walking up the back stairs. "None of you are allowed up there or in the basement until I make sure it's safe."

Totally annoyed, I grabbed my homework and headed to my room.

Plopping on my bed, I flicked on the TV. The last half of *Star Wars* was on. It was my all-time favorite movie, but I only caught the last half of it.

After that was over, I quickly got bored.

What I needed was a hobby, I decided while switching the positions of my army men on the windowsill. Any hobby, or a sport.

But it wasn't going to help me tonight. There was only one thing that would help me out tonight. And I knew what it was.

I had to get down in the basement and find that trunk stick bug had told me about.

I had totally forgotten about it until Dad reminded me.

Of course, he said going down there was off limits, I tried reminding myself of that as I pulled out my duffel bag from under my bed.

I tried reminding myself of that again as I reached into the bag and grabbed my flashlight I kept in there for emergencies.

The Basement

Going down into the basement was a hard decision. If Dad tells you not to do something, you don't do it.

There was also one exception.

It was okay if it was an emergency.

I was bored. And anyone who knew me knew that was definitely an emergency!

I waited by my door and listened closely for Laura to get into her room.

A few minutes later, I heard her door shut.

Quietly opening my door, I peeked out.

Everyone was in their room now.

Holding my breath, I tiptoed down the hall and crept down to the first floor into the kitchen.

As I opened the basement door, the bright beam from my light split the darkness.

But even with my high-powered flashlight, I still had to walk down some of the old wooden stairs to actually see below.

After about five steps, I carefully bent over and shined the light around the room.

Way spooky! Too spooky, in fact.

I was about to head back up when I made myself stop. *No, young Skywalker, face your fears*, I remembered from *Star Wars. Let the force be with you.*

The question was — was I a *Jedi Knight* or a chicken?

Just to be on the safe side, I took a few more steps then stopped and listened.

There was only silence, so I continued on.

The air felt a lot warmer than it did upstairs.

But the smell was worse than the heat.

It smelled rancid! *Like death!*

Shining my light toward the ground, I slowly slid my feet forward and brushed my hand through the air.

I wanted to be dead positive I didn't make any mistakes and accidentally stumble into any man-eating spiders waiting in their webs!

Wait! What was that?

Frozen, I listened.

Now I was hearing things.

After a couple of seconds, I continued on sliding my feet toward the back of the room and shining the flashlight from left to right.

I still couldn't really see anything.

It was just a bunch of taped-up boxes.

There probably wasn't a trunk down here anyway, I decided after stumbling around for a while. That old bat's crazy.

I felt like a fool for believing her.

"Ouch!" I hollered out as I smashed my leg into something.

Shining the light down, I saw it was just a rusty old tricycle.

I shoved it into the side of two old rotted rocking chairs, tangling my hand in a thick web.

"YUK!" I growled, dragging my hand back through, slashing the web into a million pieces.

Then something sounded like it exhaled!

I swung around, then froze!

I was positive I heard something that time.

I held my breath and listened closely.

Something *was* breathing, and it was coming from under the stairs.

I pointed my light in that direction and slowly began edging toward it.

Bending forward, I held my hand steady and shined the light through the thick wooden slats.

There was nothing under there but a black wooden box pushed up into the corner.

Wait a minute . . . that box must be the trunk Ms. Scurlock was talking about.

Seeing a rake leaning against the stairs, I grabbed it and began dragging it back and forth to clear a path — right through the disgusting thick nest of draping webs.

Getting down on my knees, I carefully scooted up under the stairs.

I tried to pull the lid open, but the key lock had been nailed shut.

Searching behind me in a pile of junk on the floor, I found a large rusty screwdriver.

I grabbed the screwdriver and jabbed it between the lid of the trunk and the lock.

As the lock began to tear from the rotted wood, I heard a loud exhale!

It came from inside the trunk!

Only this time, it was cut off by a gurgling, choking hiss!

I jumped up and stared at the trunk.

I picked up the rake and jabbed at the lid.

The lid suddenly sprang open!

Armed with the rake, I waited for a minute to make sure nothing came jumping out.

No sounds this time, so I stepped in closer.

I pointed my light down.

It was filled with shredded newspapers.

Anxiously sticking my hand inside, I poked around.

Then carefully, I began to scoop it out.

Halfway into the trunk, I still hadn't found anything except newspaper. I did notice a date on the edge of a torn corner — June 1, 1970.

It must have been locked up for a long time.

"What a rip-off!" I moaned.

There wasn't any army stuff in there.

I was about to give up when I saw the edge of something sticking out.

Reaching down inside, I pulled it out.

It looked like it was some kind of game.

I stood back up to examine it.

I almost jumped out of my skin when the lid of the chest slammed shut. I quickly dropped the game to wave the dust out of my face.

As the air cleared, I shined my light down to see **KEEP OUT** had been carved into the trunk's lid.

I hadn't seen that.

I reached down to pull the lid back open, but no matter how hard I pulled on it, it was now stuck. I couldn't even get it to budge.

I pointed the flashlight down at the game.

It was called **CREEPERS.**

"WHOA!" I yelled out, jumping back.

Something felt like it slid over my foot!

As my whole body turned into a wet noodle, I lost my grip on the flashlight.

It just slid right out of my hand.

I threw my right hand forward to catch it, but instead of catching it, I whacked it!

I watched helplessly as the flashlight went flying across the room.

It sailed forward until it hit the ground and rolled under something in the far corner.

"No way!" I groaned. I had lost my light.

I was standing there in pitch darkness!

Closing my eyes, I quickly mustered up the courage to take three big leaps toward where I had seen the light disappear.

I closed my eyes and began leaping.

I was okay until the second jump.

I tripped on something and fell right on my face! But luckily, I fell right where the light had rolled under.

Blindly throwing my hand under, I swiped it to the right. The flashlight wasn't there.

Then I bent even lower and peeked under again.

I could barely see it.

The light was dim as it had rolled into the far corner of the back wall.

I carefully reached under again and felt to the left.

Got it!

NO!

Whatever I had in my hand moved!

THUD! I heard as I slung it against the wall!

I quickly yanked my hand back!

Whatever I had grabbed scrambled around.

Then it scurried back over my foot!

And it sounded like it was hissing!

With a third — quick — try, I threw my hand back under and grabbed the flashlight.

I quickly sprang back to my feet.

I was ready to get out of there and fast!

Sailing across the floor, I grabbed the game and flew up the stairs, taking them three at a time.

Rules of an Ancient Game

Out of the creepy dungeon and back in the kitchen, I leaned against the door, panting.

I guess I should have been scared to death.

Instead, I started laughing.

Quietly, but laughing.

Well, that explains it. I'm a chicken! A ten-year-old chicken who's scared of the dark!

I was sure of one more thing, too. I deserved a medal for what I had just been through.

I sat the game down on the counter next to a plate of cookies.

I turned my flashlight to the box.

It didn't look like an ordinary board game.

First of all, the outside wasn't made out of cardboard.

It was actually faded, rough cloth that was tattered and torn covering something hard.

I ran my fingers along the worn corners.

A few loose strings hung from the edges.

There were dark, oily stains all over the top of the lid.

It must have been played many times.

Across the top, the letters looked like the old-fashioned kind. They had lots of swoops and swirls. The ones that are always hard to read.

The name **CREEPERS** was written in dark red. And the letters were still really shiny.

That was weird, especially since the game looked so old.

I ran my finger along the name again.

CREEPERS.

I flipped the game over for any instructions on the back side.

But the bottom was the same as the top.

Just the word **CREEPERS.**

Wait a minute. This must be the top. There were no seams for the lid.

I must have been looking at the bottom.

So . . . I flipped it back over again.

Okay. No seams on this side, either.

I sat the game down and stepped back.

I stood there for a minute scratching my head.

Then I picked it up again.

This time the lid slid off easily between my hands. As the bottom slid from the top, I heard a loud suction sound.

The bottom of the game fell to the counter with a thud!

Still baffled, I tried to place the lid back on the box.

I wanted to find out where the seams were.

But the lid didn't fit now.

I turned the lid clockwise and tried to put it on again. It still didn't fit.

I was about to try again when I noticed the game board inside the box.

It was like nothing I had ever seen!

It was made out of wood. No. It seemed to be some kind of metal. No. It was wood. It had to be. Things were carved into it. But it reflected the light from the flashlight like metal.

It looked brand new.

There were four little doors on each corner of the board. The doors even had tiny little doorknobs and tiny little hinges.

I pulled each knob, but they didn't open.

In the center of the board was some writing.

At the top of the writing was a symbol of the sun. I couldn't be sure, but it looked like it was made out of some type of rough stone that stuck out from the board.

At the bottom of the writing was a symbol of the moon.

The moon looked iike a little dish of water.

I went to touch the sun.

As I lowered my hand, it became warmer.

In fact, the closer my fingertips came, the hotter it got. It was so hot, I couldn't actually touch it.

Then I tried to touch the moon.

I could touch that.

Even though it looked like water, it was solid.

But when I pulled my hand back and jiggled the board, *the moon rippled!*

I couldn't wait to learn how to play it.

I had to find the directions!

That's when it hit me that the writing in the center of the board must tell you how to play.

I positioned my flashlight and started to read. It seemed to rhyme, so I read out loud.

The game of CREEPERS is a game of fright.
You only play once. You should play in the light.
All play to win. But almost all will lose.
There are no rules. And you cannot play in twos.

Now this ancient game that has been offered to you
Has fields of bright grass that shimmers green dew.
You may choose to admire it, and not play at all.
But you'll have to run fast, or through the ground you will fail.

Then around sunlit corners, you will advance so prepared,
May lie obstacles of gloom that may cause you despair.
Always the option to continue and chance by fate
You will excel through tunnels and not be consumed as live bait.

But few excel with this maze of fright.
If I were you, I would hold on tight.
For the bats that fly their best in the night,
Will trap you in caves where the bat has its best sight.

It's not a fairy tale that you'll then start to play.
No chips to count at the end of the day.
For this is the hardest part of the game.
The creatures that chase you are far from tame.

W · A · I · T
No turning back now,
you have read the directions to the game.
Now, the option is to you.
You must pass or play.

"What are you doing down here?" A voice whispered out of nowhere.

Surprised, I dropped the game and spun around.

It was just my dumb sister standing there in her stupid pink flannel pajamas.

She was holding her favorite pink pencil with pink feathers sticking out of the top.

She was just a big pink unwelcomed sight!

"Are you talking to yourself?" she asked with her normal dumb giggle.

"You didn't scare me, you know." I laughed back, trying to catch my breath. "But those ugly pink pajamas could scare anyone."

"Are you sure I didn't scare you?" she annoyingly asked me again.

"Shhh! You want to get us busted?" I said, holding my finger over my lips. "Make sure you whisper."

Then she got nosy as usual.

"What is that?" she mumbled, blowing cookie crumbs onto the game board.

"Shut your big mouth," I warned her. "It's nothing you would be interested in."

I quickly went to put the lid back on the box.

But the lid pulled right out of my fingertips.

Another loud suction yanked it back and right into place, securely covering the game!

Surprised, I stared at the box!

"Let me have that," Laura tried demanding again — pushing my arm aside, biting into two cookies at once, and blowing more crumbs across the lid of the box.

"Stop it!" I warned her again as I brushed off her mess. "It's mine. I found it first."

"You need to let me see it," she jabbered like usual.

"You need to mind your own business," I reminded her. "And you also need to go back upstairs and pop that big pink pimple you call a brain."

"I'll play it if I want to," she annoyingly griped out.

"Oh, no you won't," I warned as I walked up the back stairs — the whole way keeping the game securely guarded under my left arm.

She was the nosiest sister in the world.

I'll hide it for now, I decided.

I would play it when she wasn't around.

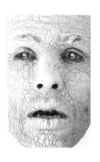

My New Best Friend

Rain was banging on my window when my alarm went off the next morning.

Staggering out of my bedroom, I saw our faithful old collie sitting in the hallway.

"Hey, Sparky," I said with a big smile.

Then I shot straight up.

Wait a minute. We don't have a dog!

"Luke, you're going to miss the bus," Mom called from downstairs.

I took a step backward and stared at the strange dog wagging his tail.

I could actually see through him!

The name SPARKY shined from his blue collar.

But for some reason, I already knew that.

I felt a hand brush up against the back of my neck.

I swung around to show Laura — only no one was there!

"What's wrong, Jelly Bean?" A strange man asked me standing at the end of the hallway.

"HUH?" I asked, rubbing my eyes.

I could . . . I could see through him, too!

"Who are you?" I asked him.

The man didn't answer.

"I've just cleaned up your mess," Mom yelled again from the kitchen.

"What mess?" I yelled back. "Hey! Who's this guy up here with this dog?"

"There's a man upstairs with a dog, huh? There better not be a dog in this house. Now hurry up. You're going to be late for school."

I turned back around and the man and the dog were now gone.

This was one day I was really happy to go to school.

Mom was mad at me for some reason.

And I was seeing things.

Things were going a little better at school. There I met my new best friend. His name is J.B.

J.B. has the blondest hair of anyone I have ever seen. It is totally white. And so is he.

His skin was about the same color as his hair. And he has these big laser blue eyes.

The guy has some gross lips, though. They are really pale, and he is always licking them.

Nasty! Very nasty!!

I think he wears the same clothes a lot, too. They seemed pretty dirty.

I guess he cares about himself the same way he cares about school. He just doesn't care.

J.B. tightened the strings to the hood of his jacket so I could only see his eyes and mouth.

Then I saw his tongue fall over his lips and make a big swipe across.

Super disgusting!

"We are exactly the opposite," J.B. said as he studied me.

"Yeah. I know." I started laughing. "You have white hair, I have dark. You are short and thin, and I am really big and tall."

J.B. looked out from under his hood. "You're not that tall."

"I am, too!" I demanded. "My grandfather told me I'm the same height he was at my age. And he's a colonel!"

"Neat-O," J.B. uttered, unimpressed.

J.B. studied me again.

"You know, you remind me a lot of my best friend in fifth grade." He continued, "He liked kickball, too. But he was a little taller than you."

"What do you mean?" I asked. "I'm the tallest kid in fifth grade. The school nurse even said so. What's his name?"

"Not this fifth-grade class," J.B. admitted as he pulled the strings of his hood even tighter.

I noticed my shoe was untied, so I knelt down to retie it.

I asked him, "That means you flunked last year? Right?"

"Right?" I asked him again as I stood up.

J.B. wasn't there anymore.

I heard Laura's voice coming up behind me.

"Talking to yourself again?" She laughed.

I snorted, then kicked a rock across the dirt on the playground. "If it's any of your business, I'm talking to my new friend J.B. And take that stupid pink pencil out of your hair."

"Look around, lizard lips. We're the only two out here," She blabbered. "Aren't you a little old to have imaginary friends?"

10

The Swarming Locust Return

The second bell rang just as I dropped my books on my desk.

Laura was sticking her tongue out at me.

I threw my tongue back at her.

"Luke! Get your tongue back in your mouth," Ms. Sabastian demanded. "Now, let's talk more about the history of our old town and the graveyard this school sits on."

I sat bolt upright in my seat!

"Can they do that?" I blurted out.

I slowly stared down at the ground.

When I looked up, I gasped.

Ms. Scurlock was now standing in the room. It was old stick bug herself!

Sternly, Ms. Scurlock told me, "Raise your hand, young man. And yes, they did that.

She laughed a strange laugh as she walked over to the skeleton hanging in the corner.

Picking up the skeletons left arm, she waved it to the class.

She looked directly at me and stopped laughing. "Makes you wonder when they move a graveyard, if they move everything."

I stared ahead at her in disbelieve!

No one was saying anything.

But everyone looked frightened.

Ms. Sabastian acted like she didn't even see Ms. Scurlock standing there.

"So, how are you, Luke?" Ms. Scurlock asked me, pushing Ms. Sabastian aside as she made her way back to my desk.

Grasping my chin with her bony fingers, she gave it a quick shake.

Seeing her fingers up close, I saw that they were really skinny and long — just like the skeletons hands hanging in the corner.

Three fingers didn't even have fingernails. They were just nubbed at the end.

"What happened to the end of your fingers?" I asked, pushing her hand out of my face.

"I've been digging," she answered.

"What are you doing here?" I asked.

"What do you expect?" she said as her beady eyes darted around the room.

Then her beady eyes stared back at me. They seemed to look right through me.

Her smile widened enough for me to see many of her yellow, grungy teeth were missing.

I shifted uncomfortably.

Then she grinned even wider.

"It's time to play, little Luke. By the way, since I'm the one who sold you the house, how do you like living there?"

"I don't like living there! There is something weird about that house. You know, like it's h-h-haunted or something," I stuttered.

"Don't be ridiculous," she said.

Then she made her eyes look more beady than they already were. "We don't like that word. Let's just say an old house comes with many little secrets. I see it's told you one."

"S-s-secrets?" I stuttered again.

Tears filled her bloodshot eyes as she said, "You know, I have a boy that's your age. He liked to play games. In fact, you're going to help him play one now. He's been playing for a long time. It's about time someone took his turn."

My whole body became limp.

Suddenly, I heard a loud flapping noise. It sounded like wings outside the classroom window.

I turned and looked out.

I couldn't see any birds. In fact, I didn't see anything that could be making the sound.

But then I noticed the playground. It was covered in bright green grass, not dirt, like I knew it was.

"Go ahead," Ms. Scurlock said, motioning toward the window.

I stared back outside.

Now I saw big hills that rolled far into the distance. They were also covered in the same bright green color — shimmering and glowing.

Wait a minute. I didn't remember those hills being there, either.

I slowly stood up and walked toward the window.

It wasn't that I wanted to. It was more like I was pulled toward it!

Everyone in class watched as I walked over.

Some of the students dropped their heads on their desks.

One girl even covered hers and whimpered.

Standing at the window, I studied the bright green grass.

Then I had the strangest urge to climb out, only I didn't have to. As soon as I pushed the window open, I was instantly pulled through!

I landed softly in the middle of a massive green field.

And as far as I could see, it was that same shinny grass that blanketed everything.

At the far end of the field, I saw a tree a monstrous tree that didn't have any leaves.

The upper branches looked like millions of skinny black fingers scratching the sky.

Then I heard a familiar voice.

It was J.B.

"What are doing out here?" I asked him.

J.B. started skipping in a circle around me.

He said, *"Now this ancient game that has been offered to you has fields of bright grass that shimmers green dew. You may choose to admire it, and not play at all. But you'll have to run fast, or through the ground you will fall."*

J.B. stopped skipping right in front of me.

He said as he tilted his head and grinned, *"Luke be nimble. Luke be quick. Luke is helping me light my candlestick."*

It was the same thing Ms. Scurlock had said!

He removed a box of matches from his pocket and handed them to me.

Then he pointed at the tree. "I would hurry if I were you."

I looked at the matches in my hand.

When I looked up, J.B. was gone.

I turned around and scanned the field. J.B. was nowhere in sight.

The only thing I could see was the tree in the distance, so I began walking that way.

With my next step, my foot plunged into a hole all the way up to my knee!

I twisted and fell.

My knee throbbed as I yanked it out.

Jumping back to my feet, I began limping forward.

Looking at my knee as I dragged it along, I began to panic when I saw that I could see through some of the grass — through empty patches on the ground!

There was no soil below for the grass to grow out of.

There was no bottom!

There was only sky beneath me!

Only holes to another sky!

With a limped jog, I staggered on, trying only to step on the solid patches of grass.

That's when I heard it. It was behind me.

I recognized the sound instantly, but I turned to look anyway.

It was the horde of hideous green scorpion bugs from my dream!

I let out a scream as I put my head down and charged toward the tree!

Leaping wildly, I tried my hardest to stay on the solid patches of grass.

The swarm got louder and louder as more joined in. *And they were zeroing in on me!*

One of the giant insects sliced through the side of my shoulder.

As I looked into its multiple eyes, through grinding fangs, it let out an oily hiss and then sped past me!

My body began to ache in pain as I ran blindly in terror, feeling the beats of their wings as they swooped down and whirled around me!

I screamed in fear when I saw the bugs hit the ground running!

They were sprinting across the grass on their two back hind legs!

The giant insects marched forward as their tentacles kept the other insect warriors at a safe distance from each other.

Many of them passed by me *hissing* and then sailed ahead!

As I slammed my eyes shut, I ran right down the middle of the insect stampede!

Then everything went silent.

The only sound I could hear was my breath coming. Ragged.

I slowly opened my eyes.

The scorpion beetles had landed, and they were now perched in the big black tree.

Terrified, I stared up at hundreds of green bugs watching me! Hissing!

Oily green goop oozed out of their green insect heads!

It was dripping down the thin branches and spattering on the bright green grass below!

Jumping backward, I tripped.

Drenched in sweat, I tumbled to the ground and rolled onto the soft green grass.

Shakily, I quickly got back onto my feet.

The tree was now gone!

The scorpion locust — gone!

I was just about to take a step forward when something fell against my leg.

Hesitantly, I looked down.

It was the tree. Only, it had shrunk!

Slowly, I bent down and picked the little tree up. It was only about a foot tall now.

Then I noticed that each of the limbs was actually the wicks of a candlestick.

I was completely confused until I looked in my hand at the matches.

I knew what I needed to do.

Quickly I opened the box.

There was only one match.

I lit the first wick, but as I went to light the next, the match went out!

I was about to panic again when I noticed that the fire traveled from limb to limb until I was holding a blazing torch.

Then I suddenly found myself standing in a dark cavern nose to nose with J.B.

"Not one from the left. Nor two from the right. Choose the right door to vacate this fright."

I didn't know if I should hug him or punch him in the face!

"What's going on?" I yelled.

Without his lips moving, I heard his voice say, *"When I am your guide, I'll walk by your side. This is the first of four. Choose the right door."*

Then he stepped back.

Directly ahead of me were three doors.

"What's going on?" I shouted.

Dropping my torch, I began shaking him by his shoulders.

The torch rolled directly in front of the door all the way to the right.

Then I noticed that the more I shook J.B., the softer his shoulders felt in my hands.

He suddenly became completely limp.

Then the hood to his jacket flipped back.

But instead of seeing his face, *I realized I was holding a jacket full of crawling maggots!*

They began to cover my hands and arms and spill in mounds all around my feet!

I heard a wet squashing noise as I pulled my right foot up out of the pile.

I kicked the mass of bugs from my feet and spun away.

I ran toward the torch, kicking it out of the way, then kicking the door open wide.

I jumped through the opening.

11

Get Out of My House!

"LUKE!"

"W-What? I don't want to play! It's not my turn! I want to pass!"

My eyes opened.

I gasped in a huge breath of air.

I was lying on a cot in the nurse's office.

The nurse, the principal, and Ms. Sabastian were all standing over me.

I'd had another dream!

I grabbed the sheet from the cot and pulled it up to my face.

It was just like the dream I'd had in the van.

Only this one was worse!

It was just a dream, though. Wasn't it?

Staring down, I saw I was still holding the match box clutched in my hand!

Ms. Sabastian turned to look at Ms. Talbot, the principal.

Ms. Talbot laughed. "He wants to pass."

Then she turned to look at Ms. Whitley.

Ms. Whitley was the school nurse.

Ms. Whitley reached down and ran her cold fingers through my drenched hair.

I heard Ms. Sabastian say, "His inner light is strong. It's expected in the beginning. But I cannot have him disrupting class anymore."

"Luke, we are calling your parents." Ms. Talbot told me as she reached for the phone.

I didn't say anything.

Fifteen minutes later, Mom ran through the office doors.

After a private conversation with the principal and the nurse, I was driven away.

We only lived ten minutes away from my school. But in that ten minutes, I couldn't answer even one of my mom's many questions.

It was only until later that night I was ready to talk.

As I walked into the kitchen, she turned back nervously to face me. "Are you okay, Luke?"

I had never seen her look so worried.

"I don't think so," I answered.

"Then tell me what happened."

"I had a nightmare," I said, pushing letters around on her desk. "Mom, I think something is trying to get me."

"What's trying to get you?" she asked.

"These huge flying bugs from my dream. And then Ms. Scurlock told me . . ."

"Ms. Scurlock?" Mom asked quickly. Haven't I told you? Ms. Scurlock's dead. She died the day we moved in."

Every hair on the back of my neck stood up!

Not from what Mom had just said, though.

I knew Ms. Scurlock was just in the dream.

I was shaking when I saw our family picture sitting on Mom's desk.

Dad wasn't in the picture anymore!

It was just Mom, Laura, and me.

Suddenly, I heard J.B.'s familiar giggle.

It seemed to be far away, then right next to me, then far away again. *"When I am your guide, I'll walk by your side. That was the first of four. You chose the right door."*

Then his ghost-like image appeared standing by the sink!

I stared at it numbly.

A single fly crawled over his lip and up his nose! He shook his head a little. Then he banged his palm against one ear as if to remove something.

"What's wrong with you?" I asked him.

The back of his hand went up to the corner of his mouth. "It's not so bad once you get used to it. But I hate the spiders. At least where they come from. You will, too."

I jumped back as a thin black snake slid out from under his hood and fell to the floor, squirming.

He picked it up by the tail and dropped it head first down his throat, licking his dry, chapped lips with a smack.

"When I am your guide . . ." he started again.

"Why are you saying that stupid rhyme?"

"CREEPERS," he whispered.

"What? What are you talking about?"

"You have to play," he whispered in my ear. "You're playing right now."

"I'm not playing anything! I've only looked at the game. I haven't played it yet!"

J.B. let out an evil laugh. "It's too late. You read the directions."

Mom grabbed me by my shoulders.

"Who are you talking to?" she asked.

"J.B.," I answered, pointing. "Can't you see him, Mom? He's standing right there!"

He walked past Mom and pulled the back of her ponytail.

I shook my head in horror!

Mom didn't even feel it!

"GET OUT OF MY HOUSE!" I cried out.

J.B. snarled at me. "You can kick me out of your house. You can pretend to ignore me. You can even call the police for all I care. But you can't get rid of me!"

As he walked toward the back door, he turned back and said, "I'll see you again, Luke. I'll see you in your dreams!"

Thunder rumbled, and all of a sudden it started getting really dark outside.

I quickly ran over to the couch and crawled under the blanket. "Mom! You gotta get us out of here! Out of this house! Out of that school!"

Mom shook her head.

I studied her doubtful expression.

"I want to help you, but we're not moving because you are having bad dreams," she told me.

"Mom, something's after me!" I yelled.

"Stop it! There's nothing after you, Luke."

"Mom, what about the storms? I bet it's not raining anywhere else — just at our house!"

"Luke, if this is your way of trying to get out of helping me around here, then . . ."

"Mom! Look outside!" I pointed.

"Honey, are you scared of storms? Let me tell you something I heard when I was your age. You don't have to be scared of thunder. It's only clouds that bump into each other."

I couldn't believe she was telling me this!

She walked over and sat down next to me.

"You know, I always heard when it rains, the angels were crying tears from above. Sometimes they cry from happiness. Sometimes they cry from sadness."

I looked right into her doubtful eyes and said, *"Well, then they really must have been upset last night!"*

Her eyebrows arched as she studied me.

"Don't you get it!" I said again. "It only storms when I'm around!"

Mom and Laura walked toward the front door.

"You're right, Luke!" Laura said as she ran back in. "It's just raining at our house."

"Okay," I heard Mom saying. "Maybe that is a little strange, but sometimes that happens. I've seen it before."

Hail started crashing against the windows.

Thunder crackled as thick bolts of lightning shot in every direction across the sky.

Mom slowly looked out the back door as she walked back into the room.

I turned back and pointed at the picture.

"What happened to Dad?" I asked her.

She stared at the picture.

Her fingers ran along the place where Dad once stood — her eyes swelling up.

Then she swung around. "You're serious about this? Are you telling me that we're in some kind of danger?"

"Yes!" I told her. "I think it's because of a game I found in an old trunk in the basement that Ms. Scurlock told me about."

"Your dad said not to go in the basement until he made sure everything was safe."

"Mom!" I yelled. "I know. But I did. And now it's too late! The game is evil! I've opened up some kind of door!"

I slowly turned and glared out the back door. "And they'll soon be coming back for me!"

71

Laura began sobbing. "Luke! You're always getting into something you shouldn't."

"Be quiet!" I yelled at her.

"Stop it!" Mom yelled. "Go start packing! We're going to Grandpa's. Bring only what you need to. We'll send for the rest later."

"You're scaring me!" Laura blubbered.

Another bolt of lightning struck.

"Get away from the window, Laura," Mom ordered.

"Why can't we leave now?" I pleaded.

"Luke, we can't leave until after school tomorrow. Your principal called me earlier and said you have to be in school tomorrow. She said you have a very important test."

"Mom! I'm not going back!"

"You have to," mom cried out. "Just take the test so that you don't get in any trouble. I promise, I'll have the van packed and ready to leave the moment you're out of class."

"MOM! You're sending me back?"

Laura started screaming at me.

But I didn't listen to a word she said.

I couldn't. I didn't care anymore.

I just held my hand tight on my forehead as my head dropped to my chest.

The Giant Lizard

"Shhh! Listen!" I held up my finger.

"What's wrong?" Laura quickly got quiet.

"Whispers. Can't you hear them?"

I slowly walked to the door and peeked out.
I stood shocked!

My entire homeroom was standing outside on my back porch! And they wear wearing *costumes.*

It was some of the strangest clothes I had ever seen, too.

A couple of the kids were in bell bottoms.

But some of the girls were even wearing old-fashioned long ruffled dresses down to their feet. One guy even had on a black cape.

Everyone stood looking inside, staring!

J.B. was standing right in the middle.

Just like before, without moving his lips, I thought I heard him say something.

Shaking my head, I took a deep breath and stared at his mouth. His lips weren't moving!

Suddenly, something popped me on the side of the head, bounced off the window, and fell right into my left hand.

It was Laura's stupid pink pencil.

"What are you staring at?" Laura asked me as she hid behind the kitchen door.

I quickly grabbed tight onto the pencil and held it in front of me.

Then Cindy, who sat next to me, walked up to the door and pressed the side of her face against the window.

"What's your problem?" I yelled through the glass.

"You better be nice to us!" She growled.

I could hear her voice inside the house!

Thunder started blasting outside. It shook the window so hard, the sliding glass door started vibrating.

All of the kids whispered at the same time, "Pass or play. Pass or play. Pass or play."

Overhead, I saw another thick, gigantic bolt of lightning strike the ground.

And then all of the lights went out!

My heart raced when I heard the glass door began to slide open!

"Pass or play," they whispered.

Just as I turned to run, my body felt like it was being pulled. Then suddenly, I was propelled backward!

Gasping for air, I began throwing my arms around frantically, now splashing around in some of the foulest smelling liquid that I have ever smelled in my life!

I let out a loud strong gag as a small beam of light suddenly appeared in the distance.

It was enough light for me to see I was now in some kind of tunnel.

Slamming my foot into the side wall, the tunnel shifted violently.

It pulled me back under, and I was suddenly sucked toward the dark end where my body jammed into a narrow section.

As light appeared again, I could see J.B. was floating in front of me on his back. "It's easier when you keep your mouth shut," he told me.

I gagged a long drawn-out gag. "What's that smell?"

"It's whatever it's been eating!" he said.

"What do you mean *IT?*" I called out.

He started laughing and said, *"Then around sunlit corners, you will advance so prepared, may lie obstacles of gloom that may cause you despair. Always the option to continue and chance by fate, you will excel through the tunnels and not be consumed as live bait."*

"This isn't happening!" I screamed.

"Then where's your dad?" He wickedly grinned. "And what about your mommy?"

"Leave them alone, J.B."

"Your mom doesn't care about you, Luke. She wants you to go back to school tomorrow. Doesn't matter anyway. You'll be spending a lot of time there now. Like forever! Just like the rest of us. Always on the run. Running for your life. **Running for the rest of time!**"

"STOP IT! It's just a dream!"

"They thought the same thing." J.B. cackled.

Suddenly the tunnel began to expand.

As the walls stretched back open, I swung around. Everyone from class was in there, too!

They were all lined up.

As the separated beams of light shined in, I could see they were being pulled one by one down into something. Pulled by the walls!

The tunnel shifted again.

J.B. fell against me.

An enormous slithering bug suddenly appeared from under his jacket sleeve!

It slimed its way up his arm and then into his open hood as he whimpered!

I watched the stomach of his jacket swell to twice its size. He grabbed ahold of his neck and said, "Just a minute."

I heard a gagging sound as hundreds of long-legged spiders spilled out of his mouth!

They scurried along the murky water and then swam their way back up his pant's legs!

There was a single spider leg twitching at the edge of his mouth. He saw the look on my face and quickly brought the back of his hand and wiped the spider leg away.

J.B. smiled. *When I am your guide, I'll walk by your side. This is the second of four. You better choose the right door!*

"Are you telling me we're in something alive?" I cried out.

He began laughing a frightening laugh. "Ever wonder what it would be like to be digested?"

His voice echoed inside the grimy walls.

"Then where are the doors?" I yelled.

J.B. slowly turned and looked toward the light at the end of the tunnel.

Of course! It had to be the way out!

That's where the light was coming from.

Holding my breath, I sank into the dark waters below and started swimming toward the light.

After about twenty strokes, I was out of air.

I splashed to the surface and gagged!

Sinking my nails into the slick bottom, I clawed my way upwards, slip sliding, shimmying along like I was climbing a pole.

Reaching the end of the tunnel, I grabbed ahold of the opening and pulled myself through.

I bounced across the concrete.

As I stared up, I was sickened!

I saw what I had fallen out of!

I had fallen out of the gooey opening of the mouth of a giant lizard!

I had been caught in its throat!

Rising high into the air, it let out a loud roar.

Then it hissed at me as its scaly body arched back!

Thunder boomed, and then — *poof* — it vanished!

Fluttering of Wings

Standing in the place of the giant lizard, the ghostly image of the strange man that I had seen upstairs appeared.

"Jelly Bean. There you are. I thought I would never find you," it said.

"Who are you?" I asked, pulling strings of slime out of my hair.

"Jim Scurlock," it answered, smiling. "You know who I am."

Mom's arm was griped tight onto Laura's shoulder as they slid back the door.

They couldn't see the ghost man.

But they must have been terrified looking at me.

They must have thought I was crazy!

Then J.B. walked out right between them!

They didn't even feel it as he walked through them! Right through their bodies!

He pointed in front of me.

There, lying on the ground, was our family picture. *And the game!*

I stared at the picture.

It had changed again!

Mom was still in it.

I was, too.

So was Laura.

But the strange man standing in front of me was in place of my dad!

And J.B. was in the picture, too!

"I know who you are now," I said to J.B. "You're Jared! Aren't you? And your last name is Scurlock! Isn't it?"

"Bingo," J.B. admitted.

"Why didn't you tell me your name before?" I asked him.

"You never asked me," he replied.

He started to look really sad.

"My real name used to be Jared Bradley Scurlock. They called me J.B. for short."

"Then . . . that means he's your dad," I said, pointing at the ghost.

"Yeah. Only we can't see each other." He frowned.

"If I can see him, why can't you?"

"I'm caught somewhere in time. In a state of limbo. He can't see me until someone takes over as the lead player in the game."

"Why does he think I'm you?" I asked.

"Ghosts can't see well, Luke. I thought everyone knew that. He just thinks you're me. He only knows that you're a boy, and he knows we're about the same age."

"But J.B., why is the picture changing?"

"He can feel that I'm coming back to him. Our family is starting to come back together. We've waited for a long time for someone like you to take over the game."

"So, I'm doomed! All because I found that stupid game in this stupid house."

"Hey, buddy," J.B. said, "I like this house. We're the people who used to live in this house."

Now it was all starting to make sense.

"That means old stick bug Scurlock is your mom!" I said slowly.

J.B. held his finger over his lips.

"Is she one of them?" I asked.

He nodded his head . . . *Yes.*

He kept his voice low. "The head and the meanest scorpion beetle is always your mother. Whatever you do, you don't want to make them mad. They'll really bite your head off! But after you start playing, they don't seem to know who you are anymore."

I quickly reached over and grabbed the game board.

Two of the four doors looked different. They looked more like a drawing than a carving. The other two doors still had tiny doorknobs sticking out.

I quickly studied the directions.

Most of the words didn't make sense — just a bunch of letters jumbled up together.

I started where I could.

But few excel with this maze of fright. If I were you, I would hold on tight! For the bats that fly their best in the night, will trap you in caves where the bat has its best sight.

"You better hurry," he said, pointing into the darkness.

I heard the fluttering of wings again.

"Is it them?" I asked, jumping to my feet.

I heard the soft buzzing of a swarm in the not very far distance.

"What do I have to do?" I quickly asked.

"You have to play," he told me.

"Can't I pass?" I asked, trembling.

"You can. But those who pass are eaten! The bugs will tear you apart limb by limb! Then they will play tug-of-war with your bones! I've seen them do it. Don't you at least want the chance to play?"

"I guess so," I grimly replied. "Playing sounds a lot better than that."

J.B. stared out at the other students.

"You mean all the other students at school have played, too?" I asked him.

"Yes. But not only the students. All of the teachers, too. It's all of the players throughout time that have lost. They let us study until it's time to play. Then the nightmare starts all over again!"

"Can you win the game?" I asked him.

A small spider crawled out from his ear.

He shook his head, aggravated.

"I doubt it. I've never known anyone who has won. Look, I've told you enough. If they find out I've told you any of this, they'll come after me for sure! You found the game. It's your turn to play. Now take my turn."

The swarm started getting louder.

They were getting closer!

"But can I win? Is there any chance?" I impatiently asked.

"Like I said, I doubt it."

So, I don't even have a choice. I have to play the game, I grimly thought to myself.

"Yes," J.B. told me.

He could read my thoughts!

"Once you lose, then you become the main player. Then I'll just become a regular student. I'll still have to play, but only sometimes. You will be the one that will be always on the run! Always waiting and hoping someone else finds the game. But that could take a long time!"

I looked at all of the other students scattered around my back yard.

Some of them were hiding behind trees.

Some of them had climbed up in the trees and were clutched onto branches.

Some of them were hiding in the bushes.

All of them looked scared out of their minds.

I felt sad for them. They were all trembling.

Then I realized, some of them must have been around for thousands of years now!

14

The Cave

The wind whistled and every window on the back side of the house began to rattle!

J.B. frowned. "Are you ready?"

"Are they here?" I asked him.

I helplessly looked at Mom and Laura.

They had been listening the whole time.

But they could only hear what I had said.

Their expressions were blank.

Mom's hand reached out for me.

J.B. grabbed hold of my arm just as the back porch gave way!

Then . . . **down we went, sliding into the blackness!**

I lost my grip on J.B. as I pitched hard and reeled as I tried to get my footing, but there was nowhere for my feet to go.

I tumbled and rolled out of control.

Suddenly my fall righted itself as my weight shifted downward. That's when I realized I was on some sort of enormous slide!

With no way to stop, I began grasping for objects, but I was falling so fast, I couldn't grab on to anything.

The slide cut sharply to the left and then slammed me back to the right.

Then almost straight down we plunged.

At times I could barely feel the slide on my back. It was more like the feeling of falling than sliding. I wanted to scream, but I knew there was no use!

Too sick to even catch my breath, I spiraled into a corkscrew.

Just when I thought it would never end, I felt a series of small bumps which slowed me down.

Then the fall evened out to a flat surface and spat me out, sending me sprawling as I rolled into a heap and finally bumped to a stop!

J.B.'s voice whispered in the darkness.

"But few excel with this maze of fright. If I were you, I would hold on tight. For the bats that fly their best in the night, will trap you in caves where the bat has its best sight."

I tried to get up when J.B. squealed, "DON'T MOVE! Wait till you can see."

I slumped back down and closed my eyes.

A minute later, I opened them.

"J.B.!" I screamed out.

I was sitting on the edge of a cliff!

I bolted to my feet — staggering backwards into the entrance of a giant cave.

"What's next?" My voice echoed.

J.B. stepped back away from me.

Behind him were a row of twenty doors.

"J.B.! Tell me what to do," I begged him.

"I can't, Luke. If I tell you the door to choose, they will eat me alive."

J.B. began walking down the line of doors dragging his hand across each of them.

He came to a stop at one particular knob.

He looked down at it, and then back at me.

Suddenly, he buckled over, screaming.

Tears burst from his eyes.

Then he disappeared!

I ran into the cave and over to the door he had left his hand on.

The dirt below was muddy with his tears.

I pushed my right foot deep into the dirt and twisted it.

Then I felt something wet explode on my shoulder and splatter up onto my cheek.

Something else exploded on the toe of my shoe.

I went to wipe the black chunky goop off my shoulder when I was struck hard in the back.

Glimpsing at what had attacked me, I saw it was a giant hairy black bat!

Flapping its way upward, it joined back with the other bats circling above me.

A small bit of sunlight flitted among them.

There were hundreds of them! A sky of bats circling right above my head!

The low screeching grew louder and louder.

I threw my hands over my ears to block out the deafening noise.

Wet goop began to rain down on me.

All at once, the screeching stopped.

There was an eerie silence.

Then there was one more long screech.

Horrified, I watched as the hairy bats began dropping from the ceiling.

They were diving straight down at me!

Covering my head with my jacket, I started to run away from the doors.

One of the giant bats slammed into me, sinking its fangs into my side, breaking into my flesh!

Beating it off with my fists, I staggered forward, then sailed into a hysterical blind run.

Suddenly I felt another sharp peck on the back of my leg, causing me to lose my balance!

Just as my feet left the ground, the bat came from under me, causing me to do a complete backward flip — landing me straddling the back of the bat's neck!

Grabbing ahold tight, I was thrust back as the bat lifted into the air and began flying out of the cave!

Out of the cave we soared! Out of the cave on the side of the cliff!

Soaring in the sky, I stared down petrified as we flew above the bright green grass below.

Then a rasping voice boomed all around me.

Loud and strong, it spoke. *"I am your guide, I'll walk by your side. This is the third of four. Choose the right door."*

My scream pierced the night sky. "I can't get to the doors!"

We began to soar even higher — higher and higher until its wings finally leveled out.

Then, suddenly we dropped — spiraling downward with me clung tight to the back of its neck! As the bat leveled out again, soared back into the cave's entrance, rejoining the other circling bats.

Then flying up to the ceiling, we suddenly jerked to a standstill!

I was now hanging upside down from the caves ceiling! Trying not to flinch a single muscle. Trying my hardest to hold on for dear life!

Low screeching filled the walls of the cave.

What am I going to do now? Did they even know I was hanging there?

I looked back down at the row of doors.

Which one was it? Which door did J.B. stop at and put his hand on?

I knew I had to decide what to do. And I knew I had to decide it fast!

That's when it hit me.

Bats dive after flying objects.

I remembered the times my friends and I would sit outside at night under the big trees at my old house throwing rocks into the air and watching the bats dive down at them.

But I needed something to throw.

Slowly sliding my right arm back into my coat pocket, I felt around. It was empty.

Then I carefully reached back to my left pocket and felt something!

It was the pencil Laura had thrown at me when I was staring out the back sliding glass door. I couldn't believe it hadn't fallen out.

Carefully pulling it out, I flailed it downward as it whistled into the darkness.

One by one, the bats let go, diving downward.

The one I had ahold of dove, too!

Halfway down, I was prepared to let go!

But I couldn't see the bottom!

As long as I could, I held out.

Then, just as the bat began to soar back up, I let go!

Hitting the ground, I tucked over then rolled to a stop right in front of the row of doors.

I had to choose, and fast! *But which one?*

Then I saw where I had angrily twisted my foot into the ground.

At the door he had vanished at when he was crying.

With one hard push, I thrust it open and jumped through!

A Ghostly Family Reunion

15

As my eyes slammed back open, I found myself back in my bedroom. I was safe.

No. I couldn't be safe yet. I had only made it through the third part of the game.

Laura suddenly came running into my room.

"Where have you been? Come on! Mom said we're leaving tonight!"

"It's no use, Laura. I can't run!"

I started to tell Laura about what happened. But I didn't.

If J.B. was telling me the truth, I didn't want to make the ghosts mad, either!

I jumped up and ran into the bathroom.

Standing at the sink, I felt a tap on my left shoulder.

My spine tingled all the way up to the base of my neck!

J.B. was standing on the left of me.

"What are you doing? Why aren't you ready?" Mom asked as she walked in and stood on my right side.

She didn't know J.B. was in there with me!

I wasn't sure what was about to happen.

Mom gasped.

"What's wrong?" I asked her.

"I can see him, Luke."

"You can?" I asked, surprised.

I rubbed my eyes and stared at J.B.

Suddenly, he started looking different.

He started looking like a normal kid.

Well, more like a normal ghost kid!

"Wait a minute. What's happening to me?" J.B. asked. Even he was surprised.

"Is that him?" Mom gulped.

Her eyes were as big as frisbees.

"Sparky!" J.B. called out.

The ghost image of the strange dog I had seen came bounding into the bathroom.

Then I saw another figure step out from behind Mom — out from the shadows.

"Ms. Scurlock?" Mom asked, surprised. "But I thought you were dead."

"I am," she answered.

The old stick bug was standing there, too, all right. But it was just her ghostly image!

"Jelly Bean, it's time to go," Ms. Scurlock said. "Bye, Luke. Thank you for everything. You brought my son back to me. I'm sorry if I scared you. I don't really remember too much of what happened, but you really are a charming little soldier."

Suddenly the ghost image of J.B.'s father walked into the bathroom, too.

Then my dad walked in, yawning. He was all right! "Wow. I must have been in a deep sleep," he said.

It was one big freaky sight.

All of us smashed into the bathroom.

My family — still alive!

J.B.'s family — all dead!

Oh, and Sparky — their dead family dog!

"Wait a minute, J.B." I suddenly realized. "Why is this happening this way? I thought you said I had to completely play the game."

"I know," he said, shrugging his shoulders. "Look. I've got to explain to my parents why I can't go with them. I'll still have to play. But at least I'm not the lead player."

Then who is? I wondered.

J.B. waved good-bye as they all disappeared into the shadows of the hallway.

"Is it over?" Mom asked.

"Yeah, Mom." I smiled. "I guess so."

Mom and I walked down the hallway together, holding hands.

"Laura," Mom yelled downstairs.

Laura didn't answer.

We walked into my room.

I heard a flapping noise at my window.

A huge lump formed in my throat!

"Oh, those pesky birds built another nest in that old oak tree."

I breathed a gigantic sigh of relief!

"It's cool, Mom. Let them stay."

Pulling my window up, I stared out.

The air smelled crisp. It smelled good.

And I felt great! I had made it through the game. Ms. Scurlock was right. I was a soldier.

Dad's voice boomed up the stairs. "Luke, come on. I need your help."

Dad's voice even sounded great.

Even if it meant having to work.

"I'm sorry I didn't believe you, Luke. I promise that next time I will."

As I turned to face her, I froze!

The lid was off the game!

Suddenly I heard Laura scream.

As I turned and looked out the window, I saw her dart across the yard.

The hoard of swarming bugs was right on her tail!

Mom ran back into the room and grabbed my hand.

"MOM! LAURA OPENED THE GAME AND READ THE DIRECTIONS!"

Suddenly Mom's hand tightened over mine, so tight it was starting to hurt.

Then her head spun around.

My heart dove into the pit of my stomach!

Standing in front of me was a corpse!

"Don't you want to play?" it rasped.

"The game's over!" I yelled, pulling away.

"No, it's not!" It let out a hideous laugh.

"But the rules said two people can't play!"

"You're twins! Twins can both play. Laura just took over your last turn. **And you better hope she wins, or I'll be coming back for you!"**

Then Mom suddenly transformed into one of the huge flying bugs, lifted her wings, and soared right out of my bedroom window!